DISCARDED

Let's Give Kitty A Bath!

STORY BY STEVEN LINDBLOM
PICTURES BY TRUE KELLEY

▲ Addison-Wesley

Text Copyright © 1982 by Steven Lindblom
Illustrations Copyright © 1982 by True Kelley
All Rights Reserved.
Addison-Wesley Publishing Co., Inc.
Reading, Massachusetts 01867
Printed in the United States of America

BCDEFGHIJK-WZ-89876543

Library of Congress Cataloging in Publication Data

Lindblom, Steven.
  Let's give Kitty a bath!

  Summary: Two children try to give Kitty a bath and a
merry chase ensues when Kitty tries to hide from them.
  [1. Stories without words.   2. Cats—Fiction.
3. Baths—Fiction]   I. Kelley, True, ill.   II. Title.
PZ7.L6573Le   [E]   81-19068
ISBN 0-201-10712-0   AACR2

To Jub the Cat

Here Kitty!

Here Kitty, Kitty!

Here Kitty, Kitty, Kitty!

Here Kitty, Kitty, Kitty, Kitty!

Here Kitty, Kitty,
Kitty, Kitty, Kitty!

Here Kitty, Kitty, Kitty,
Kitty, Kitty, Kitty!

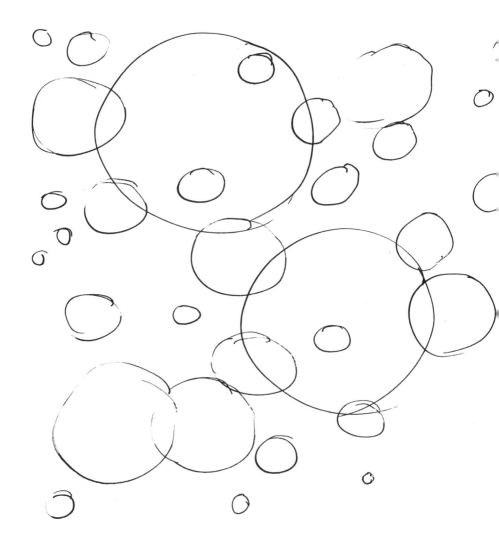